T. J. rushed back to his room and called to Zack who was still in the tree.

"Anthony and the other guys are at the door. My mom's letting them in. They want to see my snake! What should I do?"

"I don't know!" Zack called back to T. J. "Stop her from letting them in!"

"It's too late! I hear them downstairs, and I hear my mom's footsteps on the stairs!" said T. J. "What are we going to do?"

THE PET
THAT NEVER WAS

NANCY SIMPSON LEVENE

Chariot Books™
David C. Cook Publishing Co.

Chariot Books™ is an imprint of David C. Cook Publishing Co.
David C. Cook Publishing Co., Elgin, Illinois 60120
David C. Cook Publishing Co., Weston, Ontario
Nova Distribution Ltd., Torquay, England

THE PET THAT NEVER WAS
© 1992 by Nancy Simpson Levene for text and Robert Papps for
illustrations

Designed by Elizabeth Thompson
Illustrated by Robert Papps
First Printing, 1992
Printed in the United States of America
96 95 94 93 92 5 4 3 2 1

Library of Congress Cataloging-in-Publication Data
Levene, Nancy S.
        The pet that never was/Nancy Simpson Levene.
        p. cm.
Summary: Seven-year-old T.J. feels bad about lying to his classmates,
pretending to have a boa constrictor for a pet, but eventually he does
manage to acquire a pet and the knowledge that God will forgive him
if he is honest about his mistakes.
ISBN 1-55513-394-0
[1. Honesty—Fiction. 2. Pets—Fiction. 3. Christian life—Fiction.]
I. Title.
PZ7.L5724Pf 1992
[Fic]—dc20   91-33518
                                                CIP
                                                AC

To my Lord Jesus Christ
Who cuts me an abundance of His cleansing mercy,
and to my dad, Chuck Simpson,
the first "Charley" in my life and the best.

If we confess our sins to him, he can be depended on to forgive us and to cleanse us from every wrong.

I John 1:9
The Living Bible

ACKNOWLEDGMENTS

I want to thank veterinarian, Dr. Tom Hollenbeck, for his wonderful advice on German shepherds.

Thank you, Ed, for your ideas in exaggeration, your scientific knowledge, and your grasshopper elimination idea. Thank you, Patti, for your encouragement. Thank you, Cara, for your help with experiments, chapter titles, and everything else.

CONTENTS

1

MUD BALL FIGHT

"What are you bringing to show and tell, T. J.?" one boy asked from across the circle.

T. J. didn't answer. He just shrugged his shoulders. He sat on the outside of the circle of boys. It was recess time and they were discussing the family pets that they were going to bring to school to show their classmates. Mrs. Hubbard, the boys' second grade teacher, had started the school year by allowing the children to bring their pets to school.

"Well, I'm bringing my dog, Mitsy," a boy named Stephen said. "She's a real neat cocker spaniel and can do lots of tricks!"

"I'm bringing my cat, Rocky," another boy said excitedly. "My mom says she'll let me bring him in his cage, and then she'll come to the school and pick him up."

"You mean we'll get to have him in our class

the whole morning?" the others asked. "Awesome!"

"What about you, Zack? What are you going to bring?" the boys asked.

"Guess I'll bring our dog, Ranger," Zack answered. "I'd like to bring our new kitten, Smokey, but Mom says he is too little. We just got him last week."

"Well, I guess I'm stuck bringing my mom's poodle, Zsa Zsa," Aaron sighed and made a face. The other boys laughed. Aaron was a strong, husky boy who was known for his tough goal-keeping abilities in soccer. The thought of him bringing a poodle to class was pretty funny.

"T. J., you haven't said what pet you're going to bring," a boy suddenly remembered.

"Yeah, what are you going to bring to show and tell, T. J.?" the boys asked.

T. J. scowled and looked down at the ground. The truth was that he did not have a pet to bring to show and tell. Oh, he had tried and tried to get his parents to let him have a dog or a cat, but so far they had resisted the idea. "We'll get you a pet as soon as your baby sister, Elizabeth, gets a little bigger," they had said. T. J. sighed. Elizabeth was now two years old. Surely she was old enough to have a pet in the house.

"Well, what are you going to bring, T. J.?" the boys asked again.

"Uh, I'm not sure," T. J. said in a low voice. He continued to stare at the ground.

"I bet he doesn't even have a pet," jeered a boy named Anthony. Just because his mother was the leader of the boys' new Cub Scouts den, Anthony thought he should be the leader in everything the boys said or did. T. J. and his best friend, Zack, had joined Cub Scouts for the first time this year, but Anthony's behavior was almost spoiling the whole thing. "I always knew you were a weirdo!" Anthony shouted at T. J.

"I am not a weirdo!" T. J. snapped back at Anthony.

"Then tell us what pet you're gonna bring," challenged Anthony. He grinned at the other boys who began to snicker at T. J.

"WEIRDO! WEIRDO! WEIRDO!" they chanted.

Finally, T. J. could stand it no longer. "I'm going to bring a pet that's better than any of yours!" he shouted. "I'm going to bring a snake!"

The laughter and the chanting stopped suddenly. "WOW!" the boys all gasped. They looked at T. J. with new respect. Even Anthony quit his smirking.

"What kind of snake do you have, T. J.?" the boys asked as they all crowded around him.

"A boa constrictor," T. J. answered immediately. It was the most exciting and dangerous snake that he knew.

"A BOA CONSTRICTOR!" the boys shouted. "FAR OUT!"

"How long is it?" someone asked.

"Eight feet long," T. J. answered without batting an eye. He knew all about reptiles, having read about them in the set of encyclopedias they had at home. His real specialty, however, was dinosaurs. T. J. had read everything he could get his hands on about dinosaurs. It was his favorite subject.

"What do you feed your snake?" a boy asked.

"Mice," replied T. J.

"You mean live mice?" someone asked in amazement.

"Of course," someone else answered before T. J. had a chance. "The snake eats a whole mouse and then it gets a big hump in its middle."

"Oh yeah," said another boy, "and it stays that way for a few days."

The boys went on discussing snakes for the rest of the recess. T. J. quietly slipped away from the group. He felt bad that he had lied to his friends by telling them that he had a snake when he really didn't. But everybody else was talking about their pets, and he did not want Anthony to call him a weirdo. If only they hadn't bugged him so much about bringing a pet to show and tell.

T. J., whose real name was Timothy John Fairbanks, Jr., picked up a soccer ball and headed for the field. He wanted to practice a few soccer moves to take his mind off his problem. After dribbling the ball to the field, he began to work on juggling it from foot to foot. T. J. was an excellent soccer player, especially for a seven year old.

"Hey, T. J.!" a voice hollered from behind. T. J. turned to see his best friend, Zack, running onto the field.

"What are you doing down here?" Zack asked as soon as he reached T. J. "Why didn't you stay with the rest of us?"

"I dunno," T. J. shrugged and looked down at the ground. "I guess I felt kinda bad, you know, about telling everybody that I have a snake."

"Oh yeah," Zack replied. "I almost choked when you said that! You better warn me the next time you're gonna say something like that."

"I wish I hadn't said it now," T. J. admitted. He slumped to the ground and held his head in his hands. "Where am I going to get an eight-foot long boa constrictor to bring to show and tell?"

"Beats me!" Zack exclaimed. He sat down beside T. J. "Why did you tell them you had a snake anyway?"

"I dunno," T. J. groaned. "I guess I thought it would sound neat. You and the others all started talking about your pets. I just didn't want anyone to know that I don't have a pet."

"Yeah," Zack nodded. "I understand." He gave his friend a pat on the back. "Don't worry about it, T. J. We'll think of something."

After school, T. J. and Zack hurried out of the second grade classroom, down a hallway, and around a corner to the kindergarten room. T. J.'s younger brother, Charley, had started afternoon kindergarten this year. T. J. had to walk him home from school every day. Zack, of course, helped his best friend with the task.

T. J. found his blond-haired little brother waiting for him at the door. Everyone in the Fairbanks family had blond hair. T. J.'s two little sisters, Megan and Elizabeth, had blond hair, and so did his parents.

"Come on, T. J.," Charley cried as soon as he saw his older brother. "I gotta hurry. I need to do an experiment when I get home."

T. J. sighed and shook his head. Charley was

always running what he called "experiments," and usually his experiments got him into trouble. Once Charley had flooded the bathroom by trying to build a dam of mud and sticks in the bathtub. He had said that he was studying beavers. Another time he had killed one of Mother's prized orchid plants by watering it with red soda pop. Charley had thought that the red soda would make the leaves more colorful.

T. J. did not ask Charley about his next experiment. He didn't want to know anything about it. He was afraid his parents might somehow hold him responsible if he knew about the experiment before it happened.

Zack, T. J., and Charley began their walk home. Suddenly Zack had an idea. "Let's see if we can catch a snake in the creek down behind the school. Then you'll have a snake for show and tell!"

"But we couldn't catch a boa constrictor out of the creek," T. J. objected.

"Aw, who cares?" Zack replied. "At least it would be a snake. You could tell the boys that you thought it was a boa constrictor."

"Okay," T. J. agreed. Any snake was better than no snake at all, and besides, hunting for a snake sounded like a good afternoon project.

After taking Charley home and checking in with their mothers, T. J. and Zack hurried back to the school. They circled around to the back of the building and headed down toward the creek.

It was a beautiful, sunny but cool October day. The leaves had turned all kinds of colors and were beginning to float lazily off the trees. The boys crunched them under their feet as they walked.

T. J. and Zack slid down a bank to the creek and spent a few minutes swinging on the branches of a huge willow tree that grew out over the water. For many years the willow had been a favorite attraction to children exploring the creek.

Suddenly T. J. groaned and whispered to Zack. "Oh no, look who's here!" He pointed to a small group of boys who were playing further down the creek. They were boys from his class. Anthony the bully was one of them.

"Quick, hide!" said Zack. He and T. J. darted behind the trunk of the willow, but they were too late. The other boys had spotted them.

"HEY, T. J.! ZACK!" the boys hollered. "COME ON OVER HERE!"

"UH, NO THANKS!" Zack called back. "WE GOT SOMETHING ELSE TO DO!" With that, he grabbed T. J.'s arm and pulled him up the creek in the other direction.

"HEY! WHERE YA GOIN'?" the others called after them.

"SO LONG!" Zack and T. J. shouted. They ran as fast as they could, dodging rocks and jumping wet spots. Slipping and sliding along the bank, they were soon a muddy mess.

"Do you think we got rid of 'em?" T. J. finally gasped.

"Maybe," Zack replied, turning to gaze back down the creek.

"Let's hide behind those rocks and wait and see if they follow us," T. J. suggested. "I'd hate for them to catch us hunting for a snake."

"Okay," Zack agreed. The two boys climbed the bank and scrunched down behind a few big boulders where they couldn't be seen from the creek below.

It wasn't long before they heard voices from around a bend. A few moments later, three boys popped into view as they stomped along the creek bank below.

"Hurry up, Anthony!" one of the boys called over his shoulder. "We'll never catch up with Zack and T. J. if we have to keep waiting for you."

"Aw, clam up," retorted an out-of-breath and much annoyed Anthony. "I'm coming as fast as I can."

From their hiding place, T. J. and Zack watched Anthony huff and puff his way into view. T. J. had an uncontrollable desire to throw something at the bully. Digging his fingers into the mud, he quickly formed a small mud ball. He waited until Anthony was well past the rocks and up the creek several yards. Then he flung the mud ball high in the air towards Anthony.

PLOP! SPLAT! The mud ball hit Anthony's shoulder and rolled into the water beside him, splashing water all over his legs.

"HEY!" Anthony shouted, nearly falling into the creek in surprise. "Somebody threw a mud ball at me!"

"Aw, come on, Anthony," the other boys called over their shoulders. "HURRY UP!"

Grumbling and muttering to himself, Anthony stumbled a few more feet up the bank. T. J. and Zack moved out of their hiding place and quietly followed Anthony. This time Zack let a mud ball fly. KERSPLASH! It landed right in the middle of the group of boys. Zack and T. J. quickly ducked behind a bush.

"YIKES!" the boys yelled as water and slime splashed everywhere.

"I TOLD YOU SOMEONE'S THROWING MUD BALLS!" Anthony shouted rather loudly.

T. J. and Zack could not keep quiet any longer. "HA! HA! HA!" they laughed as they came out from behind the bushes.

"It's T. J. and Zack!" the other boys exclaimed. "LET'S GET 'EM!" They quickly made mud balls of their own and threw them back at T. J. and Zack.

Soon there were mud balls flying everywhere. T. J. and Zack had to work extra hard because they were outnumbered four boys to two. However, Anthony hardly counted for the other side. He spent most of his time dodging mud balls and trying to keep his balance on the slippery bank.

By the time it was all over, the boys were completely covered with mud. It dripped from their arms and legs and oozed inside their shoes. T. J. looked down. It was impossible to tell the real color of his tennis shoes. They were a sticky, gooey brown. Mud splatters spotted his face. He could even feel it in his hair.

The boys looked at each other and started to laugh. Anthony looked the funniest of them all. He had fallen on the bank so many times that there was not a clean spot on him. His shoes were so full of mud that when he walked he looked like some kind of abominable monster.

"My mother is going to scream her head off

when she sees me," Anthony told the others. "These are my new jeans."

"Uh, oh," T. J. gulped when he thought of what his mother was going to say. He was wearing what used to be a new shirt.

"Maybe we shouldn't go home," suggested Aaron. "Maybe we should hide out all night, and then in the morning tell our parents that we just escaped from a horrible kidnapper who made us sit in the mud all night."

The boys laughed. Aaron could always be counted on to say something funny, whatever the situation.

Even though they knew it was time to go home, the boys stayed and talked and played at the creek until it was really quite late. Suddenly from down the creek, they heard familiar voices calling loudly.

"T. J.!"

"ZACK!"

"Oh no!" Zack cried. "It's our dads!"

T. J. groaned. Now he was really in trouble. Not only had he ruined his clothes with mud, but he had also stayed out too late!

2

DINOSAURS FOR DINNER

A group of very muddy boys made their way back down the creek and stood in front of two rather unhappy fathers.

"T. J.!" His father took one look at him and whistled. "Wait until your mother sees your clothes!"

"What have you boys been doing?" Zack's father asked them. "Don't you know you should have been home before now?"

"Uh, yes," Zack lowered his head and stared at his muddy feet, "but I guess we were sort of afraid to come home."

"I can see why," both fathers answered at once.

The boys followed the men out of the creek and up to the school. Because it was getting dark, the fathers insisted on making sure that the other boys got home safely. T. J. and Zack and their fathers finally made their way home up Juniper

Street hill and down the other side. They turned onto a little tree-lined street called Maple. It was a short street that ended in a circle. T. J. lived in a house on the circle. Zack lived next door to T. J.

"Oh, T. J.!" Mother exclaimed when she saw his muddy clothes. "Do not step one foot into this house, young man!" She blocked the door so that he couldn't enter the house.

T. J. had to stand outside and get rinsed off with the garden hose. Then he had to pull off his muddy shoes, socks, and shirt. His younger brother, Charley, and his little sisters, Megan and Elizabeth, came outside to watch the event. It was always interesting to see their big brother get into trouble.

"Wow, T. J.! What'd you do? Take a mud bath?" teased Charley.

"It certainly looks like it," agreed Mother. "I think you must have worked pretty hard to get that dirty."

As he poured creek water out of his shoes, T. J. tried to explain the joys of a mud ball fight, but he didn't have much success. When he was finished, his mother continued to stand in front of him with her hands on her hips and a frown on her face.

"Hmmmmph!" was all she replied. She led

him inside and steered him through the house to the bathroom where he jumped into the shower. Mother took T. J.'s blue jeans, which weren't really very blue anymore, back outside to Father who was rinsing the dirt out of T. J.'s clothes and shoes with the garden hose.

After his shower, T. J. hurried downstairs to join the family at the dinner table.

"Well, you certainly look better," Mother said to T. J. as he took his usual seat to the left of Father and beside his two-year-old sister, Elizabeth. Across the table from T. J. sat four-year-old Megan. Next to Megan sat Charley.

"You looked pretty gross when you came home, T. J.," Charley told his older brother.

"Yeah, gross!" agreed Megan.

"GWOTH!" shouted Elizabeth, imitating her brother and sister.

Everyone laughed.

"I will have to agree with that," said Father. "I think I rinsed enough dirt out of T. J.'s clothes to plant a garden!"

There were more laughs.

T. J. quickly finished his bowl of beef stew and asked for another. His adventures at the creek had made him hungry.

Charley, on the other hand, was not the least

bit interested in food. He jumped out of his chair and ran over to a set of switches on the wall.

"Is everyone ready for the experiment?" Charley asked.

"What experiment?" Mother and Father asked with alarm creeping into their voices.

"Let me guess," said T. J. "You're going to turn off the lights and see who can eat beef stew the fastest in the dark."

"No," Charley gave his older brother a scornful look. "AND NOW, LADIES AND GENTLEMEN," he declared in his very best announcer's voice, "WATCH CLOSELY! THE GREAT EXPERIMENT

IS ABOUT TO BEGIN!" With that, Charley flipped the switch that controlled the ceiling fan above the dining room table.

WHOOSH! The blades of the fan began to whirl at top speed above their heads. Immediately small items flew from the fan and landed on the table.

SPLASH! PLOP! SPLAT! Some of the items fell into the bowls of beef stew, and some landed in the children's milk glasses.

T. J. fished something brown out of his glass of milk. It was a miniature plastic dinosaur. "Hey!" he exclaimed with surprise. "This is part of my dinosaur collection."

Megan and Elizabeth squealed with laughter as dinosaurs flew around the room and fell into their bowls of stew. Mother sat speechless and stared wide-eyed at her younger son.

Father jumped up from the table and switched off the ceiling fan. "Would you mind telling me the meaning of all this, young man?" he asked Charley. Father only said "young man" when he was pretty upset.

Charley hung his head and said in a low, almost whisper-like voice, "I guess the experiment didn't work."

"You mean to tell me that dropping dinosaurs

into our beef stew was an experiment?" Father exclaimed.

"Yes," Charley answered. "You see, we were studying centrifugal force in kindergarten today. Our teacher swung a bucket of water upside down and around and around and the water never fell out. Then she let the kids try it. It was really neat. No matter how many times we swung the bucket up over our heads, the water never fell out."

"Very interesting," said Father, "but what does that have to do with dinosaurs falling into our dinner?"

"Well, I thought centrifugal force would keep the dinosaurs from falling off the fan when it turned around," Charley explained.

Father, Mother, and T. J. looked at each other and exploded with laughter. Megan and Elizabeth joined in, and even Charley began to smile.

Father pulled Charley close to him and set him on his lap. "Let's see if I can explain centrifugal force to you," said Father. "You see, most objects do not want to move. When water is put in a bucket and the bucket is swung around in circles, the water doesn't want to move out of the bucket. But because the bucket is moving, the water has to move. As the bucket is swung around, it keeps changing the direction that the water would move. This change or force keeps the water in its place. The faster you swing the bucket, the better the water stays in its place. It's just like the force that keeps people inside a roller coaster when it goes upside down.

"Now, when you put your dinosaurs on top of the fan blades," Father continued, "they didn't want to move either. But they were not put in anything like a bucket. So when they fan blades moved, the dinosaurs did not move, and PLOP! they fell to the table."

"Oh," Charley nodded his head, "so what I need to do is put some buckets on the fan blades."

"No!" said Father. "You will not put buckets or anything else on the ceiling fan. Do you understand?"

"Yes," replied a disappointed Charley.

"What I want to know," T. J. suddenly joined the conversation, "is why you had to use my dinosaurs?"

"I dunno," Charley shrugged.

"Well, you shouldn't have gotten them out of my room," T. J. scolded his younger brother. "They belong to my dinosaur collection."

"T. J.'s right," Father told Charley. "You are not supposed to play with his things unless you ask him first. Those are the rules."

"Now my dinosaurs are all yucky," T. J. said disgustedly. He held up a brontosaurus. Stew broth dripped from its feet and tail.

"Oooey gooey," giggled Megan and Elizabeth.

"Your dinosaurs will wash off, T. J.," said Mother. "Now let's finish our dinner."

The next day at school, T. J. watched gloomily as two children showed their pets to the class. One girl brought her cat, and one of the boys brought his dog.

"When are you going to bring your snake to school?" the group of boys asked T. J. at recess.

"I dunno," T. J. shrugged and tried to walk away. The group followed him.

"We want to see your snake, T. J.," they said.

"I'm beginning to wonder if he really does have a snake," said Anthony with a sarcastic grin.

That made T. J. mad. "Of course I have a snake!" he snapped at Anthony. "My dad, uh, just might not let me bring it to school, that's all. He, uh, says it's too dangerous."

"Aw . . . " the boys all sighed with disappointment.

"Hey, maybe we could come over and see it at your house," one of them suggested.

"Yeah, can we?" they all cried.

"Well, uh, maybe," T. J. stammered. "I'll, uh, have to ask my dad first."

Later that afternoon Zack and T. J. leaned against a windowsill in T. J.'s room and looked out at a tree limb. It had grown so close to the window that the boys were sure they could reach it.

"Let's unhook the screen and try to get a hold of that branch," suggested Zack.

"I don't think my parents would like that," replied T. J.

"Aw, they'll never know," his best friend assured him. "I know how to take out screens and put them back in again."

"So do I," said T. J. "I helped my dad wash the windows."

"Okay, then let's do it," Zack said. "We'll put the screen back in right away."

"Okay," T. J. agreed.

The boys yanked and pulled until they finally got the screen out of the window. It made quite a bit of noise, but T. J. did not think his mother would hear. She was on the first floor and his was the only bedroom on the third floor of the house. It was a loft bedroom, high above the rest of the house.

"Look! I told you we could reach the tree limb!"

cried Zack. He leaned far out of the window and caught hold of the nearest branch. T. J. stuck his head out of the window and looked down at the backyard below. It was three whole stories to the ground.

"You better watch out," T. J. warned Zack. "You'll probably kill yourself if you fall."

"I'm not gonna fall," Zack said. "They don't call me the 'tree climbing champ' for nothing."

T. J. frowned. He didn't remember anyone calling Zack the "tree climbing champ." He held his breath as he watched his reckless friend climb up on the windowsill, take a good hold of the branch, and swing himself over to the tree.

"See!" Zack called triumphantly to T. J. "Nothing to it! Now it's your turn."

Just then T. J. heard the door bell ring. He thought he heard familiar voices at the front door.

"Wait a minute," T. J. said to Zack. He ran out into the hallway and listened at the top of the stairs as his mother talked to whoever was at the front door.

"Can we come inside and play with T. J. and Zack?" said a voice at the door. T. J. made a face. It was Anthony.

T. J. didn't wait to hear any more. He rushed

back to his room and called to Zack who was still in the tree.

"Anthony and the other guys are at the door. My mom's letting them in. They want to see my snake! What should I do?"

"I don't know!" Zack called back to T. J. "Stop her from letting them in!"

"It's too late! I hear them downstairs, and I hear my mom's footsteps on the stairs!" said T. J. "What are we going to do?"

3

FIREFIGHTER'S RESCUE

T. J. tried not to panic, but he had to do something, fast. His mother was on her way up to his room, the screen was off his bedroom window, and Zack was perched just outside the window in the old oak tree. To make matters worse, Anthony and his friends were downstairs waiting to see a pet snake that T. J. did not have.

T. J. quickly lowered the blinds that hung over his window so his mother couldn't see Zack in the tree. T. J. then ducked behind the bed just seconds before she entered the room.

"T. J. . . ." Mother began as she reached the doorway to his bedroom. "Now, that's funny," T. J. heard her say. "I wonder where those boys have gone."

Mother's footsteps grew softer as she made her way back down the stairs. T. J. crept out into the hallway and listened as she told Anthony and the group of boys that he and Zack were not home. Then the telephone rang, and Mother went to answer it.

"Whew!" T. J. gasped. He rushed back into his bedroom and over to the window. He pulled up the blinds. "All's clear!" he called to Zack. "My mom's on the telephone so we're safe for a while."

"Good!" replied Zack. "Now you can come out here."

"Huh?" T. J. said. "You want me to get in the tree with you? Why don't you come back through the window?"

"I can't come back through the window," Zack told him. "There's nothing to hold onto."

T. J. saw that Zack was right. Going from the window to the tree was not a problem because there was a stout limb to grab, but going from the tree to the window was much more difficult. The window had only a tiny ledge that would be almost impossible to hold onto. The only way Zack could get out of the tree was to climb down.

"You better come over here," Zack insisted. "It's gonna look awfully funny if you're inside and I'm outside when we're supposed to be together. Besides, your mom thinks you're outside now. What are you going to tell her when she finds you inside? Are you going to tell her that you hid behind the bed when she came looking for you?"

"No," T. J. answered. He sighed. Zack was right. The only thing he could do was follow his friend down the tree to the ground. If only it weren't so far from the ground.

T. J. stood up on the windowsill and prepared to reach across the open space to the tree. Just don't look down, he told himself.

Just as he was about to take the dangerous leap, an arm came out of nowhere, wrapped itself around his waist, and pulled him backward into the room!

It was Mother! "DON'T YOU EVER DO THAT AGAIN!" she told T. J. rather firmly. She did not let go of him right away. Holding him tightly, she whispered, "Thank You, Jesus." She finally let go of him and hurried to the window.

"Zack! Can you climb down to the ground?" Mother called out the window.

"I think so," Zack called back.

"Then start now, but go very slowly and carefully," Mother told him.

"How did you know Zack was in the tree?" T. J. asked his mother.

"Our neighbor across the street, Mrs. Marquette, just telephoned," answered Mother. "She was on her way out to her car and happened

to look up and see Zack in the tree. She thought it looked awfully dangerous, so she called me."

T. J. nodded. So that was the telephone call his mother got right after Anthony and the boys left.

Mother and T. J. stuck their heads out the window to watch Zack begin his long climb down to the ground. It was slow going. The branches of the old oak tree were very spread out. Most of them were too far apart for Zack to reach. He had to grip the trunk and slide from one to another.

About a third of the way down, Zack ran into trouble. He had come to a fork in the tree where no smaller branches grew. For several feet, there was nothing to hold onto but the gnarled old trunk.

Zack waited for a few minutes to catch his breath and muster up his courage, then he started the long downward slide, gripping the trunk as tightly as he could. His arms did not reach completely around the trunk, however, and he soon found himself plunging down the tree much more quickly than he wanted to go.

Mother and T. J. held their breath as they watched Zack slide. He finally came to an abrupt halt when his foot hit a conveniently located knot in the trunk. Mother and T. J. breathed a sigh of relief.

"ZACK!" Mother called from the third story window. "ZACK, ARE YOU ALL RIGHT?"

Zack did not answer. T. J. looked down from the window at his best friend who hung onto the trunk of the tree for dear life. Zack looked so small in that big old tree. For the first time in his life, T. J. realized that he could never replace his best friend. Oh, he might make other friends, but they would never be the same as Zack.

"Please, Lord Jesus," T. J. prayed. "Please don't let Zack fall."

"ZACK!" Mother hollered louder this time. "ARE YOU OKAY?"

"NO!" came a muffled reply.

"ZACK!" Mother yelled again. "ARE YOU STUCK? DO YOU NEED HELP?"

Mother and T. J. waited. Finally they heard a faint cry of "HELP!"

"Oh dear!" Mother exclaimed. She backed out of the window. "T. J., stay here and talk to Zack. Tell him that help is on the way."

"Okay," T. J. replied, "but where are you going?"

"I'm going to call the fire department!" Mother called over her shoulder as she ran down the stairs.

"The fire department!" T. J. exclaimed. "Awesome!" He rushed back to the bedroom window. "HEY, ZACK!" he hollered. "DON'T WORRY! THE FIRE DEPARTMENT'S COMING TO RESCUE YOU! YOU'LL PROBABLY GET ON THE NEWS AND BE FAMOUS AND EVERY-THING!"

It wasn't long before T. J. heard sirens in the distance. As they drew closer and closer, Mother rejoined T. J. at the window. She smiled at him encouragingly. Zack would soon be rescued.

A small crowd of neighbors had gathered around the bottom of T. J.'s tree. T. J. saw Anthony and his friends among them.

Zack's mother was there, and so was his father.

T. J.'s mother had called them at work, so they both came home right away. T. J.'s own father had just been called and was on his way home from work.

Red lights flashed and sirens wailed as a fire truck, two police cars, and an ambulance pulled onto Maple Street and followed each other around the circle to T. J.'s house. T. J. whistled. The entire circle was filled with bright lights and men scrambling from their vehicles.

Mother hurried downstairs to talk to the firefighters. T. J. followed right behind her. He wondered if there were any reporters or photographers in the crowd.

The firefighters had set up a net around the bottom of the tree by the time T. J. and his mother got outside. Another group of firefighters leaned a tall ladder against the tree, then one of them scrambled up the ladder. T. J. had never seen anyone climb a ladder so fast!

When the firefighter reached Zack, he strapped him to his back and quickly came back down the ladder. The rescue took less than two minutes. The people on the ground clapped and cheered as the firefighter handed Zack over to his parents.

When Zack was safely back with his parents, T. J.

looked around at the crowd that had gathered. He spotted a television cameraman who was filming the rescue. T. J. couldn't believe it. He clapped his hands with excitement. Zack and T. J.'s tree would be on the news tonight!

T. J. raced over to tell Zack the good news, but he stopped short as soon as he reached him. Zack, his tough, always-ready-for-anything friend, was clinging tightly to his father's neck and sobbing uncontrollably. Zack's father and mother quickly carried him home.

T. J. felt a hand on his shoulder. He looked up to see his own father standing behind him.

"What's wrong with Zack?" T. J. asked. "Why was he crying?"

"I think Zack had been so scared for so long that when it was finally over, he just let go and cried tears of relief," Father answered. He knelt down beside T. J. and pointed up at the spot where Zack had been stuck. "After all, that's a long way up there," he said.

"Yeah," T. J. nodded in agreement.

"Your mother just told me something very disturbing," Father raised his eyebrows at T. J. "She said that she caught you just as you were getting ready to go out of the window and into the tree."

T. J. didn't answer. He just stared at the ground.

"Son, that's a long way down to the ground. It would be very easy to slip and fall." Father looked at T. J. with concern in his eyes. "Your mother and I don't want anything bad to happen to you."

"I know," replied T. J.

"Please promise me that neither you nor any of your friends will ever climb out of your window again," said Father.

"I promise," said T. J., "and I'm sure Zack will never want to do it again."

"I think you're right," smiled Father. He took T. J.'s hand. "Come on. Let's go put your screen back in the window."

4

SNAKE TALES

Zack was quite a hero the next day at school.

"We saw you on the news last night, Zack!" the other children said as soon as T. J. and Zack entered the school building.

The boys could talk about nothing but the daring rescue when they were at morning recess. Of course, Anthony talked louder and longer than anyone else. Since he watched the actual rescue, Anthony thought of himself as the expert witness. T. J. did not mind, however. He hoped Zack's episode in the tree would make the other boys forget about the snake he didn't have.

The excitement of the tree rescue lasted for a few days, but it wasn't long before the boys were asking T. J. about his snake again. They pestered and pestered him about it until T. J. could hardly stand it.

"I told you already that my dad thinks it's too

dangerous to bring a boa constrictor to school," T. J. told the group of boys.

"Then let us see it at your house," said Anthony.

"Well, maybe . . . " T. J. hesitated. He did not know what to say.

"You better not go to his house," Zack jumped to T. J.'s rescue. "His snake is really mean and hates visitors."

"You mean you've seen it?" the boys asked eagerly.

"How big is it?" one of them wanted to know.

"Oh, it's huge!" Zack was enjoying himself. "It's twelve feet long!"

"I thought it was eight feet long," said Anthony.

"It grew," replied Zack, "and it's really mean!"

"Aw, we're not afraid," Anthony scoffed. "It's in a cage, isn't it?"

"No," T. J. answered. "It's not in a cage."

"Really?" the boys looked amazed.

"Where do you keep it then?" one of them asked.

"I bet it's loose in the basement," someone joked.

"I can just see T. J.'s mom going downstairs to do the laundry and CHOMP! She gets it right in the leg!" Anthony shouted and limped around, holding his leg.

The other boys all laughed.

"That's not true!" T. J. hollered above the laughter. "It's not loose in the basement. It's, uh, in a box. My dad's, uh, making a cage for it. So you can't come over until the cage is finished."

"When will it be finished?" the boys asked.

"Not for a long time," answered T. J.

"I think I'm gonna ask your mom about this snake," Anthony said. He was getting very suspicious. "I don't believe that you really have a snake."

"Well, I do," retorted T. J., "and you can't ask my mom."

"Why not?" Anthony taunted.

"Because she doesn't know about it," replied T. J. hotly.

"She doesn't know about it!" Anthony repeated, looking even more suspicious. "You mean you have a twelve-foot boa constrictor in the house and your mom doesn't know about it?"

"Yeah, my dad and I are keeping it a secret until we can build the cage," T. J. told him. "We can only work on it when my mom's not there. That's why it's taking so long."

Anthony did not know what to say to that. It sounded possible. He glared at T. J. for a while, and then he shrugged his shoulders. "My mom would probably throw my dad and me out if we brought a twelve-foot boa constrictor into the house without telling her," he muttered. He turned to go, but then stopped and asked T. J. one more question. "What's the name of your snake, anyway?"

That question caught T. J. off guard. For some reason, all he could think of was the name of the dinosaur that had fallen into his bowl of stew the night Charley had run his disastrous experiment.

"My snake's name is Brontosaurus," he told Anthony.

"Awesome!" the boys approved of the name. The conversation quickly turned to a discussion of their favorite dinosaurs.

T. J. breathed a sigh of relief. He had managed to put the boys off again. But for how long?

"Hey, Charley, how about helping me talk Mom and Dad into getting a pet?" T. J. asked his younger brother after school one day.

Charley did not answer. He didn't even seem to have heard the question. He was standing in his room, punching holes into the top of a shoe box.

"What are you doing?" T. J. asked, coming into the room. It was hard to get Charley's attention when he was busy with a project.

"Huh? Oh hi, T. J.," Charley looked up briefly from his important work.

"What are you doing?" T. J. repeated as he stared at the mess his brother was making of the shoe box top.

"Punching out air holes," Charley replied and frowned at T. J. as if that should have been obvious.

At the risk of sounding even more stupid, T. J. asked another question, "What are you going to put in the box?"

"Grasshoppers," Charley answered.

"Grasshoppers?" asked T. J. "What are you going to do with a box of grasshoppers?"

"Study 'em," the kindergartner answered. "Do you want to help me catch them?"

"Okay," T. J. agreed. He had nothing better to do. His friend, Zack, was busy running errands with his mom.

"Well, come on," Charley had finished the box. "Let's go."

T. J. followed his brother outside, and they went down two short neighborhood streets to a small park. Charley promptly knelt down on the grass and spread a rather large net on the ground.

"Hey!" T. J. cried. "Is this our basketball net?"

"Yeah," Charley admitted. "I needed it for my

grasshopper experiment. Don't worry. I'll put it back later."

T. J. sighed. How did he get such a scientific little brother? He wondered if Charley was going to be the kind of kid who sets up a laboratory in the basement and then risks blowing up the whole house and family every time he tries an experiment.

There were plenty of grasshoppers in the park, and soon they were hopping all over Charley's net. When the net was full, Charley signalled T. J. and the boys folded the corners of the net to the middle, trapping the grasshoppers inside. They then slid the net full of grasshoppers into the shoe box and pulled it out to leave the insects behind. Charley quickly slammed the lid on the top of the box.

When they got home the boys circled around to the back of the house and went in through the family room door. Being careful not to let Mother see them, they hurried down the steps to the basement play room. Mother would not understand the need to bring a box of grasshoppers into the house.

Unfortunately, when they got downstairs they found their small sisters, Megan and Elizabeth, playing with their dollhouse.

"What's in there?" four-year-old Megan pointed to the shoe box.

"None of your business," answered T. J. gruffly. Megan annoyed him. She was always poking her nose into other people's things.

He and Charley carried the box to the other side of the basement. Megan followed. She tried to peek under the lid.

"LEAVE IT ALONE!" Charley roared. Megan turned and ran back to the dollhouse.

Just then Mother called the girls upstairs. It was time for their favorite television show. T. J. and Charley were glad to see them go.

"I think you need a better container for your grasshoppers," T. J. told his brother as soon as they were alone. "This shoe box isn't safe from Megan."

"Yeah, I know," said Charley, "but what can I use?"

"We could make a cage," T. J. suggested. "There's some screen and some wood in the garage."

"Great idea!" Charley exclaimed.

The two boys ran to the garage. They decided to leave the box of grasshoppers in the basement. They figured that the box would be safe since they'd only be gone for a few minutes and Megan

and Elizabeth were busy watching television.

T. J. and Charley grabbed a few pieces of wood and a roll of wire screen from the garage. They were heading back downstairs to Father's work bench in the basement when they heard loud screams erupting from the family room.

The boys dropped the wood and screen and ran to the family room as fast as they could go. What T. J. saw when he got there almost made him laugh. If he had not thought about the trouble he might get into, he would have howled out loud.

On the floor in front of the television lay the

shoe box. The lid was off, the box was empty, and the floor was thick with jumping grasshoppers.

Megan and Elizabeth were standing on the sofa jumping from one foot to the other. They screeched every time a grasshopper hopped in their direction. Mother had grabbed the broom and was swinging it at the insects, but T. J. could see that she was fighting a losing battle. The grasshoppers were definitely winning this war.

T. J. and Charley looked at each other and groaned. They were in for it now.

5

THE GREAT GRASSHOPPER WAR

"DON'T JUST STAND THERE!" Mother shouted to T. J. and Charley over the screams of Megan and Elizabeth. "GO GET THE VACUUM CLEANER!"

Mother took another swipe at the grasshoppers with her broom. By now all the furniture in the family room was covered with the jumpy, leggy creatures.

T. J. and Charley ran for the vacuum. As they were pulling it out of the closet, the front door opened and in walked Father. T. J. and Charley ran past him pushing the vacuum cleaner as fast as they could go.

"What's going on?" Father called after them.

"Sorry . . . we can't stop to explain . . . we gotta hurry," T. J. called over his shoulder.

T. J. and Charley rounded a corner and rolled the big machine into the family room. T. J. got on his hands and knees and searched for an electrical outlet. He found one and plugged in the vacuum. When he stood up, his father was standing right behind him, not looking especially happy.

"Get your sisters out of here," Father ordered with a grim face. He turned on the vacuum and rolled the machine forward.

T. J. pulled Megan off the couch and Charley got Elizabeth. They took the girls into the kitchen where they brushed two grasshoppers off of Megan and one off of Elizabeth. They threw the insects outside.

"All right," Charley turned to Megan. His eyes shone with anger. "What's the big idea of letting the grasshoppers out of the shoe box?"

"I just wanted to see what was in it," Megan replied as she stuck out her lower lip.

"You mean you wanted to mess with my stuff!" Charley hollered at her. "Now see what you've done? You've ruined everything!" He was so angry that he raised his hand to slap her.

"Charley!" T. J. caught his brother's hand. "Don't hit her. We're already in enough trouble with Mom and Dad."

"But she's always getting into my things," Charley complained.

"I know," T. J. agreed. He glared at Megan.

"You're nothing but a trouble maker!"

Megan looked from one brother to the other. She stuck her lower lip out even further and began to cry. Two-year-old Elizabeth soon did the same thing. Both girls sobbed and sobbed, making an awful racket.

"I can't stand it!" Charley covered his ears. "Lock them in the bathroom or something."

"I can't lock them in the bathroom," T. J. almost laughed at his brother's remark. "What would Mom and Dad say?"

"Well, get them to stop crying!" Charley pleaded.

"How?" T. J. asked. He tried everything. He made funny faces at the girls. He tried tickling them, but that only made them cry harder. It wasn't until Charley got down on his hands and knees and barked like a dog that a smile broke out on Megan's face. Elizabeth smiled too.

When Mother and Father returned to the kitchen, T. J. and Charley were barking loudly and chasing the girls around the room.

"I have one question," said Father, interrupting the chase. "Where did all those grasshoppers come from?"

T. J. and Charley looked at each other and hung their heads.

"I guess we brought them in," T. J. answered softly.

"But Megan brought them upstairs and let them out of the shoe box!" Charley added. "We were going to make a cage for them."

"Did you ask your mother if you could bring a box of grasshoppers into the house?" Father asked Charley.

"No," Charley admitted.

"Then it was wrong to bring them inside in the first place," said Father.

"Yeah, but Megan . . . " Charley began.

T. J. poked his brother. "Be quiet," he said. "You're only making it worse."

Father sighed. "I want it understood," he said sternly as he looked at all four of his children, "that no one is to bring any kind of insect or animal into this house without permission from me or your mother."

"Okay," they all nodded in agreement.

"And Megan," Father addressed his daughter, "you are to leave your brothers' things alone. It that clear?"

"Yes," Megan nodded.

"Then I declare that the Great Grasshopper War is over," Father smiled. "Let's all get ready for dinner."

T. J. and Charley looked at each other in amazement. That was it? That was all Father was going to say? They were sure that they would be punished for causing such an uproar. Sometimes you just couldn't figure out grown-ups.

Later that evening T. J. climbed up and sat on the arm of his father's chair. He sat on the arm of the chair so that no one could accuse him of actually sitting on his father's lap. After all, he had a big brother image to maintain.

"Dad," T. J. leaned against his father's shoulder, "I've been wondering about something."

Father put down the book that he was reading.

"What's that?" he asked T. J.

"Well, I've been wondering why you didn't get mad at Charley and me for bringing grasshoppers into the house," said T. J.

"Are you disappointed?" Father asked T. J. "Do you want me to punish you?"

"Oh no," T. J. replied quickly.

Father laughed and put his arm around T. J. "Do you know what it means when someone says, 'I'm going to cut you some slack?'"

"Yeah," T. J. nodded. "It means you're going to go easy on them."

"Right," said Father. "Well, in this instance I'm going to cut you some mercy."

"Cut me some mercy?" T. J. frowned. "I've never heard that before."

"You haven't?" Father looked surprised. "God does it all the time. When people are truly sorry for something wrong they have done and ask God for His forgiveness, through His great mercy He forgives them. You could say that He cuts them some mercy. I was just trying to imitate my Father in heaven and cut you some mercy."

"Yeah, I see," smiled T. J. He hugged his father around the neck. "Thanks for cutting me some mercy," he whispered.

T. J. and Zack hurried home after school the next day. They had to get ready for their soccer game that afternoon. Aaron was with them too. He was going to ride to the game with T. J. and Zack.

T. J. got more and more excited as he put on his red and white jersey, red shorts, red and white socks, shin guards, and tennis shoes. He would put on his black soccer shoes when he got to the field. He loved to play soccer. It was by far his favorite thing to do. He and Zack were center forwards, and Aaron was the goalkeeper.

"Hey, you guys! Hurry up!" Zack yelled. He was always the first one ready and was waiting impatiently for them.

"Coming!" T. J. cried. He and Aaron bolted down the stairs and out the door. The boys almost collided with T. J.'s father who had come home early from work for the game. Father flattened himself against the wall so he would not get trampled.

T. J., Zack, and Aaron kicked a ball to each other to warm up for the game. Before too long T. J.'s parents came outside with Charley, Megan, and Elizabeth. Charley wore sunglasses and a wide-brimmed canvas hat. A pair of plastic binoculars hung around his neck.

"What are you supposed to be?" Zack asked Charley with a grin.

"I'm an explorer, like David Livingston," replied Charley.

"Who?" Zack looked at T. J. with a very puzzled expression on his face.

T. J. shrugged.

"David Livingston was a very famous explorer in Africa," Charley told the older boys.

"Where'd you get that hat?" T. J. asked his brother.

"It's Dad's fishing hat," said Charley. "He said I could wear it."

"Looks like it fell in the water too many times," said Aaron.

The older boys laughed. They hopped into the back of the van. Charley, Megan, and Elizabeth sat in the middle seats.

When they got to the field, the boys ran to join their teammates who were already warming up. Their team was called the Wildcats. They were dressed in red and white. The other team was called the Rockets. They were dressed in blue. Both teams were at the top of their division. This was going to be a good, close game.

The whistle blew to start the game. T. J.'s team had won the toss so the Wildcats kicked off. Zack tapped the ball to T. J. Just as he had seen older players do, T. J. turned and quickly shot the ball backward to a halfback. Then he and Zack bolted straight up the field and waited for the halfback to kick the ball up to them.

The halfback, however, missed his first try. He was suddenly surrounded by seven or eight Rockets players and a few of his own players, all kicking wildly at the ball. There was such a tangle of feet and legs that the ball could hardly be seen. Somehow the ball made its way down the field toward the Wildcats' goal, but Aaron, the goalkeeper, was able to run out and grab it before anyone could score. With a powerful throw, Aaron flung the ball over the heads of the rest of the players. The ball bounced towards T. J. and Zack who were still waiting up field.

T. J. dribbled the ball up the center of the field and got it past two defenders before the rest of the players caught up with him. T. J. quickly passed the ball over to Zack who made a hard shot on goal. The ball hit the left goal post and just missed going in. It bounced back onto the field not far from T. J.

T. J. was ready. He smashed it back towards the goal. The ball went right between the legs of the Rockets' goalkeeper.

SHREEEEEE! the referee blew his whistle. GOAL!

The goalkeeper for the Rockets glared at T. J. "You just try that again and see what happens," he threatened.

"Don't worry, we will!" Zack called to the goalkeeper. He put his arm around T. J.'s shoulders as they walked back to the center of the field.

"I guess he didn't like my goal," T. J. grinned at his best friend.

"Yeah," laughed Zack. "Let's do it again!"

"Okay!" T. J. replied. He listened to the cheers of their fans. They were cheering for him! He had scored the first goal of the game!

This time the Rockets kicked off. T. J. and Zack found themselves in the middle of a crowd of players all trying to kick the ball at the same time. No sooner did one team kick the ball one way, then someone from the other team smashed it back again. The players ran back and forth in a zigzag line up and down the middle of the field. Finally someone chipped the ball over the other players' heads. It moved dangerously close to the Wildcats' goal.

Aaron was ready for it. With a head-first dive toward the ground, he stopped the ball and wrapped his arms around it. Cheers again rang out from the Wildcats' parents.

Aaron punted the ball back into play to the left side of the field. Then it happened—the funniest thing T. J. had ever seen at a soccer game.

The ball bounced past all the players and out of bounds into the spectators. It soon came back onto the field, being pushed by the biggest German shepherd that T. J. had ever seen. He was pushing the ball in front of him with his nose!

"Hey, that dog's got the ball!"

"Quick! Let's try and catch him!"

Shouts went up all over the field. Parents and children swarmed onto the field and tried to catch the dog that had stolen the soccer ball.

The dog seemed to think that it was a great game of keep away. He was doing a great job of avoiding the many hands that tried to stop him. The referee lunged at the dog but only managed to trip and roll on the ground.

T. J. and Zack were laughing so hard their sides hurt. T. J. thought the dog had a great break-away style and was telling that to his friend when Zack suddenly yelled, "LOOK OUT!" T. J. turned around and saw the dog racing full speed towards him!

"YIKES!" T. J. screamed as he was knocked to the ground by the huge German shepherd.

6

A DOG NAMED SERGEANT

T. J. was flat on his back. He squeezed his eyes shut and threw his hands over his face as the big German shepherd bounded over his head. T. J. figured that the dog would keep right on going, but when he opened his eyes he had a big surprise. The dog was leaning over him, his black, shiny nose almost touching T. J.'s face.

T. J. lay very, very still. At first he felt afraid, but then he realized that he was looking up into the most warm, gentle brown eyes he had ever seen. T. J. smiled and said, "Hi, boy!"

The dog wagged his tail and gave T. J.'s face a great big lick. Then he pushed the soccer ball up against T. J.'s right arm.

T. J. wiped his face with his shirt and sat up. He put his arm around the big dog's neck. "Thanks for the soccer ball," he said.

Father and Mother ran over to T. J. They were

followed by the referee and the dog's owner, an older-looking woman who looked more like she should own a poodle named Fifi than a huge German shepherd.

"Are you all right, T. J.?" Mother asked anxiously, peering at her son.

"Oh, sure," T. J. replied. "This is a really neat dog!"

"I'm so sorry," the older woman apologized to them all. "Sergeant loves to play soccer. He couldn't resist grabbing the ball when it sailed past his nose. I'm afraid he got away from me."

They all laughed.

"Sergeant is a good name for your dog," said Father. "He certainly took command of the soccer ball."

They laughed again.

"Sergeant got his name in the army," the woman told them.

"You mean he's been in the army?" T. J. asked.

"He was born into the army, you might say," the woman smiled. "Sergeant was one of a litter of pups belonging to my son's best friend. He was a sergeant in the army, and my son Tom named the dog after his friend. Tom spent a lot of time with Sergeant, so he's a very well-trained dog."

"Cool!" T. J. exclaimed. "Sergeant's like a real army dog! Your son must be really glad to have such a neat dog."

"Well, he was glad," the woman replied sadly. "You see, he was killed in a car accident not long ago."

"Oh, I'm so sorry," Mother and Father both replied.

"It's all right," replied the woman. "I am slowly learning to live with it. I thought I would want to keep Sergeant because Tom loved him so, but it's not fair to the dog. He's much too big for me to handle, so now I'm looking for a good home for

Sergeant." She smiled a little. "Besides, I don't play soccer."

"Can we keep him, Dad?" T. J. blurted, unable to keep still any longer. He wanted the dog more than he wanted anything else in the world.

"Uh, how old is Sergeant?" Father asked.

"He's four years old," said the woman. "He's a very smart dog and quite lovable."

Father looked at Mother. T. J. held his breath. Then his father, who was always very practical, said, "I think we had better talk it over."

"Awwwwww," T. J. frowned and kicked the dirt in front of him. Then suddenly he had an idea. He turned his back to everyone and said a quick prayer, "Please Lord Jesus, help Mom and Dad to want to keep Sergeant. Amen."

The grown-ups and Sergeant returned to the sidelines. The referee blew his whistle and the game continued.

Almost immediately the Rockets scored their first goal of the game. However, Zack soon made a goal off of a pass from T. J. The score was Wildcats two, Rockets one.

The Rockets scored another goal in the second half which tied the game. The score stayed tied for a long time. Then finally, near the end of the game, T. J. was able to move the ball down the field and try for a long shot on goal. He missed. The ball bounced in several directions around the goal area and eventually came back to T. J. It took a high bounce, and without really thinking about it, T. J. hit the ball towards the goal with his forehead. The Rockets' goalie was not expecting anyone to head the ball and could not get his hands up in time to stop it from sailing into the net.

SHREEEEEE! went the referee's whistle. He held his arms straight up. GOAL!

T. J. laughed in delight. That was the first time he had scored by heading a ball.

After T. J.'s goal, the Rockets seemed to lose their enthusiasm for the game. Their goalkeeper made a few critical mistakes, and the Wildcats scored twice again before the game was over. The final score of the game was Wildcats five and Rockets two.

T. J., tired but happy, walked off the field with Zack and Aaron. T. J. was opening a can of root beer when he heard his mother ask, "Where's Elizabeth?"

Turning towards his mother's voice, T. J. saw Charley and Megan returning from the playground area that was several yards away from the soccer field. Charley and Megan were alone. Elizabeth was nowhere to be seen.

"You were supposed to be watching Elizabeth,"

Mother reminded Charley. "She went with you and Megan to play on the playground."

Charley spread his arms out wide with a look of total surprise. "She disappeared," he told Mother. "She was with us a minute ago."

"Well, we had better go find her," Mother replied. She and Charley headed toward the playground. T. J. and Megan stayed behind with Father. He was talking with the older woman who owned Sergeant, and they were exchanging telephone numbers. T. J. hoped with all his heart that Father would decide to take the dog.

"Couldn't we just take him home today?" T. J. asked his father. He knelt beside the big dog and put his arm around his neck.

"Your mother and I need to discuss it first," Father replied.

"Didn't you discuss it during the game?" T. J. frowned.

"We couldn't very well talk about the dog and watch you make all those goals, could we?" Father grinned at T. J.

"But . . . " T. J. began. His plea was cut short when Mother came running from the playground.

"Elizabeth is missing!" she gasped between breaths. "I can't find her anywhere. We're going to have to call the police!"

7

A FURRY HERO

T. J. and Father just stared at Mother. What did she say? Elizabeth was missing? Call the police?

Father was the first to come to his senses. "Now, now," he tried to calm Mother. "We'll all go look for Elizabeth. Don't worry, we'll find her."

Mother nodded. She and Father walked to the playground, calling Elizabeth's name loudly. The rest of the children, Megan, Charley, T. J., Zack, and Aaron, followed. The older woman and the dog were right behind them.

"Where was the last place you saw Elizabeth?" Father asked Charley as soon as they had reached the playground.

"I dunno," Charley shrugged and looked at his sister, Megan. She, likewise, shrugged her shoulders.

"Was Elizabeth with you when you were playing on the playground?" Father tried again.

"We didn't play on the playground," Charley told him.

"Then where did you play?" Father asked. He was starting to sound a little annoyed.

"We weren't playing," Charley replied. "We were exploring like David Livingston."

"Then where did you go exploring?" Father raised his voice. By now he was more than a little annoyed.

"Over there," Charley pointed to a group of trees that stood several yards away from the playground.

"Oh no!" Mother exclaimed, covering her mouth with her hand. She hurried off in that direction.

"I thought you and Megan were told to stay in the playground area," Father reminded Charley sternly.

Charley nodded and looked at the ground.

"Come on. We'll discuss it later," Father told him. He and Charley quickly followed Mother to the trees. The others hurried after them.

The family and friends searched and searched for Elizabeth among the trees. Charley showed them his David Livingston camp, the small grassy area underneath the branches of an old willow tree. A small creek ran beside the willow and wound its way downhill into a field of grass that was part of what looked like an old abandoned farm. Only an old barn and part of a fence remained standing.

"You don't think she went down there, do you?" T. J. asked his parents. He shaded his eyes from the sun and pointed down the hill towards the barn.

"Oh, surely not," Mother exclaimed.

"She might have followed the creek down that way," considered Father, also shading his eyes from the bright afternoon sun.

The woman with the dog moved closer to Father and Mother. "If you have something that belongs to Elizabeth, we could let Sergeant sniff it. He's a pretty good tracker."

Father raised his eyebrows in surprise. "We'd be very grateful if Sergeant could help us find Elizabeth." He turned to Mother. "Do you have anything of Elizabeth's with you?"

Mother searched her pockets and came up empty.

"I do!" Megan suddenly shouted. She held up a pink hair ribbon. "Elizabeth asked me to hold her hair ribbon."

Father took the ribbon and held it up to Sergeant's nose. "I know it isn't very much," he told the dog, "but it's all we have."

The big dog sniffed both sides of the hair ribbon. He then wagged his tail.

"Sergeant," the woman said to the dog. "Go find Elizabeth!"

Sergeant cocked his ears and looked at the woman intelligently.

"Go find Elizabeth," the woman repeated.

"WOOF!" the dog answered and sprang into action. With his nose to the ground he sniffed all around the wooded area and then took off down the creek bank. Everyone followed him.

"Do you think this will work?" T. J. heard Mother ask Father.

Father shrugged. "It's worth a try," he said.

Sergeant led them in a zigzag manner along the creek. Once he waded into the water and sniffed all around the bank. Then he bounded out of the creek and continued through the field, heading towards the old barn.

The people who followed Sergeant could see nothing that told them that Elizabeth had gone that way. All they could do was trust Sergeant's nose and follow him. T. J. hoped with all of his heart that Sergeant knew what he was doing. For one thing, T. J. wanted to find his baby sister. Even though Elizabeth could be a pest sometimes, he did not want to lose her permanently. For another

thing, if Sergeant found Elizabeth, T. J. hoped his father would be so grateful that he would let T. J. keep the dog.

At last they all reached the old barn. Sergeant sniffed carefully around the entrance while the people peered inside.

T. J. started to step inside the old building, but Father stopped him. It was a good thing that he did. When T. J. looked down, he saw that the floor had completely rotted out. T. J. looked down and saw nothing but a dark, gaping hole.

"Ohhhhh!" wailed Mother. "What if . . . ?" She choked and could not finish her sentence, but they all knew what she meant. What if Elizabeth had fallen into that hole?

"We don't know that for sure," Father tried to reassure Mother. He leaned over and peered down into the hole. "Before anyone tries to go down there to look for Elizabeth," he said, "I think we had better do something we should have done at the beginning of this search."

"What's that?" they all asked.

"Pray. We had better ask our heavenly Father for guidance," he replied.

They all knelt down on the grass outside the barn door.

"Dear Father in heaven," Father started, "we ask You for help in searching for Elizabeth. We know that You have Your eye on her right now. Please guide us to her. We pray in the name of Your Son, Jesus. Amen."

As soon as Father finished his prayer, Sergeant began to bark. T. J. looked around. He had almost forgotten the dog. Sergeant had disappeared right after leading them to the barn entrance. Now his bark seemed to come from behind the barn.

"Dad," T. J. said, "Sergeant is barking."

"I know, son," his father replied. "He's probably chasing a rabbit or something."

Father stood up and went over to the gaping

hole. He stared at it intently.

"But Dad," T. J. pulled on his father's arm. "It sounds like Sergeant wants us to follow him again."

"That is Sergeant's most urgent bark," said the older woman coming up to stand beside them. "He only barks like that when he has discovered something."

"All right, we'll go see what Sergeant has discovered," said Father.

They walked around the far corner of the barn and looked out upon the countryside. Sergeant was standing several yards away in the middle of a sea of tall grass. As soon as he saw them, he began to bark furiously.

"T. J., go see what he wants," ordered Father.

T. J. ran as fast as he could to the dog. When he reached him, his heart leaped with joy. Elizabeth was sitting on the ground at the dog's feet with her favorite baby doll lying beside her. As soon as she saw T. J., her eyes grew round with excitement. "Doggy!" she exclaimed and pointed up at Sergeant.

T. J. didn't wait to hear any more. Scooping up Elizabeth, he hollered at the top of his lungs. "MOM! DAD! SERGEANT FOUND ELIZABETH!"

Mother and Father ran to T. J. and Elizabeth. For the first time in his life, T. J. saw his mother run faster than his father. She grabbed Elizabeth out of T. J.'s arms and hugged her tightly. Then Mother did something that absolutely astonished all of them. She handed Elizabeth to Father, got down on her knees, and wrapped both arms around Sergeant's furry neck.

"Thank you for rescuing my little girl," she told the dog. Sergeant gave Mother's nose a big lick in return.

"Now can we keep Sergeant?" T. J. asked his father eagerly.

Father chuckled as he looked down at Mother who still had her arms wrapped around the big dog.

"I think we'll have to," he observed, "your mother seems very attached to him."

"Best dog in the world!" Mother declared.

"YIPPEE!" T. J. hollered and began to jump around with joy. He was finally going to get a dog.

When they got back to the parking lot, Sergeant said goodbye to the older woman and then joined his new family in their big eight-seater van. The dog sat in the back seat with T. J. and his friends, Zack and Aaron. Charley and Megan leaned over the middle seats to pet him.

"I think you're more excited to get Sergeant than you are to have Elizabeth back safe and sound," Mother teased the group of children.

"Well," said Charley, looking very serious, "you can't pet a little sister."

Father and Mother laughed.

"We're glad to have Elizabeth back," T. J. assured his parents. "By the way, Elizabeth," he turned to his baby sister, "why did you run away?"

"Huh?" Elizabeth peeked around the side of her car seat to look back at him.

"Why did you go away all by yourself?" T. J. tried again.

"Baby sleepy!" Elizabeth answered. She held up the doll that she always carried.

"Do you mean you went to give your baby a nap?" asked T. J. He rolled his eyes at his friends.

"Yeth," replied Elizabeth with a serious face. "Baby sleepy!"

"But why did you have to go so far away?" Charley asked Elizabeth.

Elizabeth didn't answer. She snuggled back down into her car seat.

No one ever really found out why Elizabeth had disappeared, but no one really cared. The important thing was that she had been found and had been rescued by a big furry German shepherd named Sergeant.

T. J. hugged Sergeant. He finally had a dog, and his dog was a hero!

8

CUTTING MERCY

As soon as Father got home, he called the newspaper office and told the reporters the story of how Elizabeth had been rescued by Sergeant. A photographer from the newspaper came out that very evening and took some pictures.

In the morning, pictures of Elizabeth and Sergeant covered the front page of the newspaper.

"FAR OUT!" T. J. shouted when he saw the paper.

The telephone immediately began to ring and did not stop. It seemed as if everyone had seen the picture in the paper and was calling them about it. Even T. J.'s friends called.

"Totally awesome!" said Zack.

"That was a great picture of Sergeant," Aaron told T. J.

T. J.'s soccer coach even called. He said, "Sergeant is a dog of many talents. Not only can he dribble a soccer ball, but he rescues lost children as well. Bring him to the next game, and we'll make him an official member of the team!"

There was so much excitement in the house that morning that T. J. forgot to get ready for school. He really had to hurry when Zack came to the door.

"I saw the picture of your sister and your dog in the paper this morning, T. J.," Mrs. Hubbard said as soon as T. J. and Zack entered the classroom. "Would you bring your dog to show and tell tomorrow so we can all meet him?"

"Sure," T. J.'s face broke into a wide grin. To be able to bring a dog to show and tell had been T. J.'s biggest wish. Now it had come true! Suddenly he remembered that he had asked the Lord to help him get Sergeant. Well, the Lord had certainly come through for him.

"Thank You, Lord Jesus," T. J. prayed silently. "Thank You for Sergeant."

Most of the day was great for T. J. He was the center of attention at school. Everyone talked about Elizabeth's rescue. In fact, that seemed to be the most popular subject of the day. But later in the day during afternoon recess, Anthony said something that caused T. J.'s day to turn upside down.

The group of boys had just finished a quick game of soccer. They were walking back to the school building and talking about Sergeant's great rescue when Anthony said, "Gee, T. J., now you have two fantastic pets!"

"Huh?" T. J. responded, somewhat puzzled.

"Yeah, you know, you have a dog and a snake," Anthony reminded him.

"Oh, uh, yeah," T. J. quickly looked down at the ground so no one would see his red face.

"Some guys have all the luck," Anthony grumbled as they walked inside the classroom.

Anthony's remark bothered T. J. for the rest of the afternoon. When he got home from school, he did not go outside to play with Zack. Instead, he and Sergeant curled up on his bed. T. J. felt uneasy. He had a feeling deep down inside that he needed to tell the truth about the snake, but he was afraid to do it.

If I tell Anthony and the boys that I never really had a snake, they'll hate me and call me a liar, T. J. thought to himself.

Still, no matter how much he did not want to, he knew that God wanted him to tell the truth. After all, God had given him a wonderful dog. Surely T. J. could obey Him and admit the lie that he had told his friends.

T. J. sighed, plopped onto the bed, and thought and thought. Sometime later a knock sounded at his door.

"Come in," T. J. called.

"Hello," Father said, coming into the room. "Your mother tells me that you've been in your room by yourself all afternoon. Is there anything wrong?"

"Well," T. J. hesitated. He didn't want to tell his father about the lie. Still, his father was always very good at solving problems, and T. J. was tired of wrestling with this one by himself.

"Okay, I guess I'll tell you," T. J. finally replied.

"Okay," said Father. He sat down on the bed beside T. J. and Sergeant.

"It all started like this," T. J. began. "All of the other kids in my class at school were bringing their pets to school for show and tell. I didn't have a pet to bring, so I made up this story about having a pet snake. . . . "

T. J. went on to tell his father how he had told all the boys in his class that he had a pet boa constrictor and how the boys had tried to come and see it on the day that Zack was rescued from the tree. He also told his father that the boys thought Mother did not know about it and that Father was building a secret cage.

"And the story kept getting crazier and crazier," T. J. finally ended.

Father nodded his head. "That's what happens when a lie is told," he said. "A lie will not stand by itself. It has to be supported by other lies, and pretty soon you find yourself all tangled up in a big bunch of lies. Only the truth will stand by itself."

"I wish I hadn't told the lies," T. J. admitted. "I feel bad about them now, and I think that God wants me to tell the truth."

"I'm sure He does," Father agreed. "God hates lies. In the Bible God says that telling lies is just as bad as murdering someone!"

"Really?" T. J. exclaimed.

"Yes. God hates all kinds of sin equally. He doesn't think that one kind of sin is worse than any other. It's all bad to Him."

"Wow," T. J. breathed. He felt more worried than ever.

"There is a way to set things right with God," Father told T. J.

"How?" T. J. asked eagerly.

"You must confess your sin to God and ask Him for His forgiveness," answered Father.

"Really?" T. J.'s face brightened. "Is that all I have to do?"

"Yes," nodded Father, "but you have to really mean it."

"Oh, I do," replied T. J. "I wish I'd never told those lies."

"Then why don't you set it straight with God?" suggested Father. "I'll pray with you."

"Okay," said T. J. He bowed his head and closed his eyes. "Dear heavenly Father," he prayed out loud. "I'm sorry that I told those lies about the snake. Please forgive me. Amen."

"Amen," repeated Father. He smiled at T. J. "Now you are forgiven. God promises that He will always forgive you when you confess your sin and ask for His forgiveness."

"Yeah," T. J. smiled back at his father. "God just cut me some mercy!"

Father laughed. "You're right," he agreed. Then his face became serious again. "There is one more thing that would be good for you to do," he told T. J.

"What's that?" T. J. asked.

"You need to set things straight with your friends," answered Father.

"Yeah, I know," T. J. looked down at the floor and sighed, "but I bet they won't cut me any mercy."

The next morning T. J. took Sergeant to school. Mother went along with them. She was going to take Sergeant back home after show and tell.

T. J. sat at his desk and eagerly waited for Mrs. Hubbard to call on him. Sergeant waited by his side. He was a well-behaved dog and sat patiently, ignoring the whispers and giggles all around him. Finally Mrs. Hubbard stood up and spoke to the class.

"Children," she said, "we have with us a most honored guest. T. J. has brought his dog, Sergeant, to see us. He is the dog who rescued T. J.'s little sister and who had his picture in the newspaper yesterday. T. J., would you bring Sergeant forward so we can all see him?"

T. J.'s eyes were shining with excitement and his cheeks were turning just a little bit red as he led Sergeant to the front of the class.

"This is my dog, Sergeant," T. J. spoke proudly. He had memorized a little speech for this occasion. "Sergeant is a really neat dog. He likes to play soccer and even joined in one of our games. It kinda made the referee mad." The class laughed.

"Sergeant is also really smart," T. J. went on. "He's been very well trained. That's why he was able to find my little sister, Elizabeth." T. J. told the class all about Elizabeth's rescue. When he was finished, the whole class, even Mrs Hubbard, applauded for T. J. and his dog, Sergeant.

Red-faced, T. J. returned to his seat. He was very proud and very happy. His show and tell had been a great success.

Sergeant stayed at T. J.'s side until time for morning recess. Then Mother took the dog home. T. J. and the boys waved good-bye to Mother and Sergeant.

"You sure have a neat dog, T. J.," said one of the boys.

"Yeah," said Anthony, who had managed to position himself next to T. J. in the center of the group. "Like I said before, some guys have all the luck."

"Uh, there's something I have to tell you guys," T. J. decided then and there to confess his lie and get it over with. He swallowed hard and blurted, "I never really had a snake."

The boys all stared at him. No one spoke.

T. J. went on awkwardly, "Uh, I made up the whole thing about having a boa constrictor. I'm really sorry."

"Aw, that's okay, T. J.," a boy in the group replied.

"Yeah, who cares about a dumb ole snake," said someone else.

"Not when you have a dog like Sergeant," added Anthony. "Can we come over to your house and play with him sometime?"

T. J. couldn't believe his ears. His friends were actually cutting him some mercy. He was so grateful for his friends' forgiveness that he even put an arm around Anthony's shoulders. "Sure," he said, "come over any time."

As they all moved toward the soccer field for a quick game, T. J. smiled to himself. "Thank You, Lord Jesus," he prayed silently. "Thank You for making it all turn out right."

Amen.

Adam Straight to the Rescue

Ketchup on pancakes?

Adam has always wanted brothers and sisters . . . but this ready-made family isn't quite what he had in mind. Three-year-old Jory is cute enough, although his fascination with meat-eating dinosaurs can get out of hand. But ten-year-old Belinda is another story. How can Adam put up with a sister who calls his mother E. S. (short for Evil Stepmother), makes up stories just to scare him, and eats ketchup on everything?

"When we get back from our camping trip," his mom assures him, "it'll seem like we've been together forever." Adam's not so sure, although the two-day trip packs enough adventure to last most families a lifetime. And in spite of—or maybe because of—runaway cars, midnight animal visitors, and trips to the emergency room, Adam does some serious thinking and praying about what it means to be a brother. As he says, "I don't know why I argue with You, God. It's hard work. And besides, You always win!"

K.R. Hamilton lives with her husband and kids in Birmingham, Alabama. She has worked as a ranch hand, a lumberjack, a census taker, and an archeological surveyor, among other things. She's not likely to run out of things to write about.

Adam Straight and the Mysterious Neighbor

Listen to the "Spider Lady"?

Adam isn't sure he wants to do yardwork for Miss Winters. She lives in a run-down old house on an overgrown lot, doesn't want him knocking on the door, and warns him to stay out of the fenced-in backyard. And now a strange man in a black suit calls her the Spider Lady! Something creepy is going on here.

But Adam needs the money, thanks to his stepsister Belinda's latest successful attempt to get him into trouble. And working with his new friend, Pelican, will be fun. But before Adam even realizes how it happened, he's become something of a spider himself—spinning a web of half-truths and misunderstandings that make Belinda even angrier and may cost him Pelican's friendship.

Before the mystery is solved, Adam finds that he and Belinda aren't so different after all . . . and that God's forgiveness is something a Christian needs—and can count on—time and time again.

K. R. Hamilton lives with her husband and kids in Birmingham, Alabama. She has worked as a ranch hand, a lumberjack, a census taker, and an archeological surveyor, among other things. She's not likely to run out of things to write about.

Project Cockroach

"We'll go down in Jefferson School history."

That's what Ben Anderson promises when he gets Josh to agree to his plan. And turning loose a horde of cockroaches in Mrs. Bannister's desk drawer does sound impressive. Josh knows what Wendell, his peculiar next-door neighboor and classmate, would say, but what would you expect from a kid who actually goes to the library in the summertime?

Josh's mom wants him to be a good student and stay out of trouble. His long-distance dad back in Woodview wants him to "have a good year." Wendell wants him to go to church. But Josh isn't sure that even God can help him find answers to the questions in his life. He just wants to make a few friends and fit into his new world . . . even if it means taking a risk or two.

ELAINE K. McEWAN, an elementary school principal and the mother of two grown children, knows a lot of kids like Josh.

Chariot Books™
David C. Cook Publishing Co.

The Best Defense

"You sure know how to make a mother worry."

Josh has lived in Grandville barely two months, and he's already met the paramedics, the police, some teenaged would-be thugs, and a long-haired leather worker named Sonny. No wonder hismom gets a little anxious from time to time.

Josh thinks karate lessons would take care of some of his worries, but they aren't likely to help his relationship with Samantha Sullivan, teh bossiest kid in the fifth grade. And they won't make his dad call more often.

Sonnly tells him the key to conquering his fear is prayer . . . but Josh isn't sure that prayer is the answer. He needs to explore the possiblility. What if it doesn't work in a dark tunnel when he's facing two thugs?

ELAINE K. McEWAN, an elementary school principal and the mother of two grown children, knows a lot of kids like Josh.

Chariot Books®
David C. Cook Publishing Co.